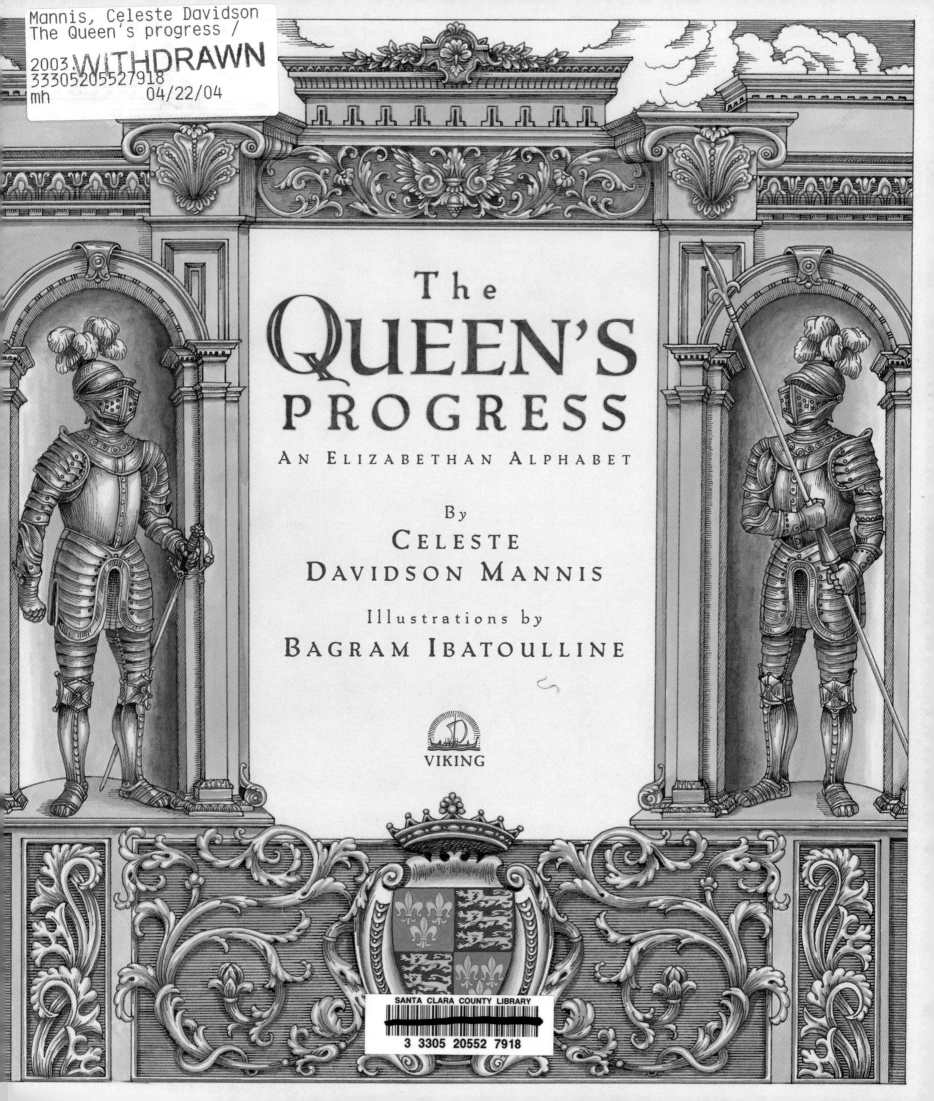

The QUEEN'S PROGRESS

An Elizabethan Alphabet

By

CELESTE DAVIDSON MANNIS

Illustrations by

BAGRAM IBATOULLINE

VIKING

Even the queen is obliged to take
a holiday from her cares and woes.
But there's no such thing as a simple escape
as every good subject knows!

So pack up a knapsack with apples and cakes
and a fresh change of clothes for the road.
Unmask the traitors in Elizabeth's wake,
as on royal progress we go!

An A for adventure.
Our spirits are high!
Fare thee well London.
All's ready. Let's fly!

EVERY SUMMER Queen Elizabeth took a holiday known as the royal progress. The queen, her courtiers, and hundreds of attendants left London in a caravan that stretched as far as the eye could see. As they passed through the gates of the city and into the country-side, only the queen knew where their rambles would lead. She was the sole navigator of the royal progress, and her whims were her compass.

B is for bear
who gambols and capers.
He begs by the carts
of the dressers and drapers.

THE QUEEN'S possessions filled more than four hundred carts. Trunk after trunk contained her traveling wardrobe, renowned for its glittering gowns and jewels. She also traveled with her own bed, bed linens, furniture, draperies, silver plate, dishes, and a portable altar.

Elizabeth was an excellent rider and preferred to travel by horseback. Poor roads, uncertain weather, and occasional diversions made progress slow, and the queen's caravan seldom advanced more than ten or twelve miles a day.

C is for crown.
The queen rules the day.
She wades through the crowd,
to her guards' great dismay.

THE ROUTE of the progress was dotted with charming villages and bustling market towns. Wherever the queen stopped, enthusiastic crowds welcomed her. Elizabeth loved to greet her subjects and accept their gifts. She was as gracious to her humblest countrymen as she was to her nobles—perhaps more so, as she was quite rude to her courtiers when it suited her. Her "common touch" earned her the undying admiration of her people.

D is for dancers sporting ribbons and bells. The maid and the page wish to frolic as well.

SPEECHES, PERFORMANCES, and pageants were planned in honor of the queen wherever she stopped. Elizabeth sat dutifully through each program but was particularly pleased when Morris dancers were part of the festivities. They performed regional folk dances and made music with bells hung from their wrists and ankles. Some masqueraded as Robin Hood and his band of merry men and reenacted the stories of Sherwood Forest.

E is for England,
isle of our story.
Its green hills and dales
are Elizabeth's glory.

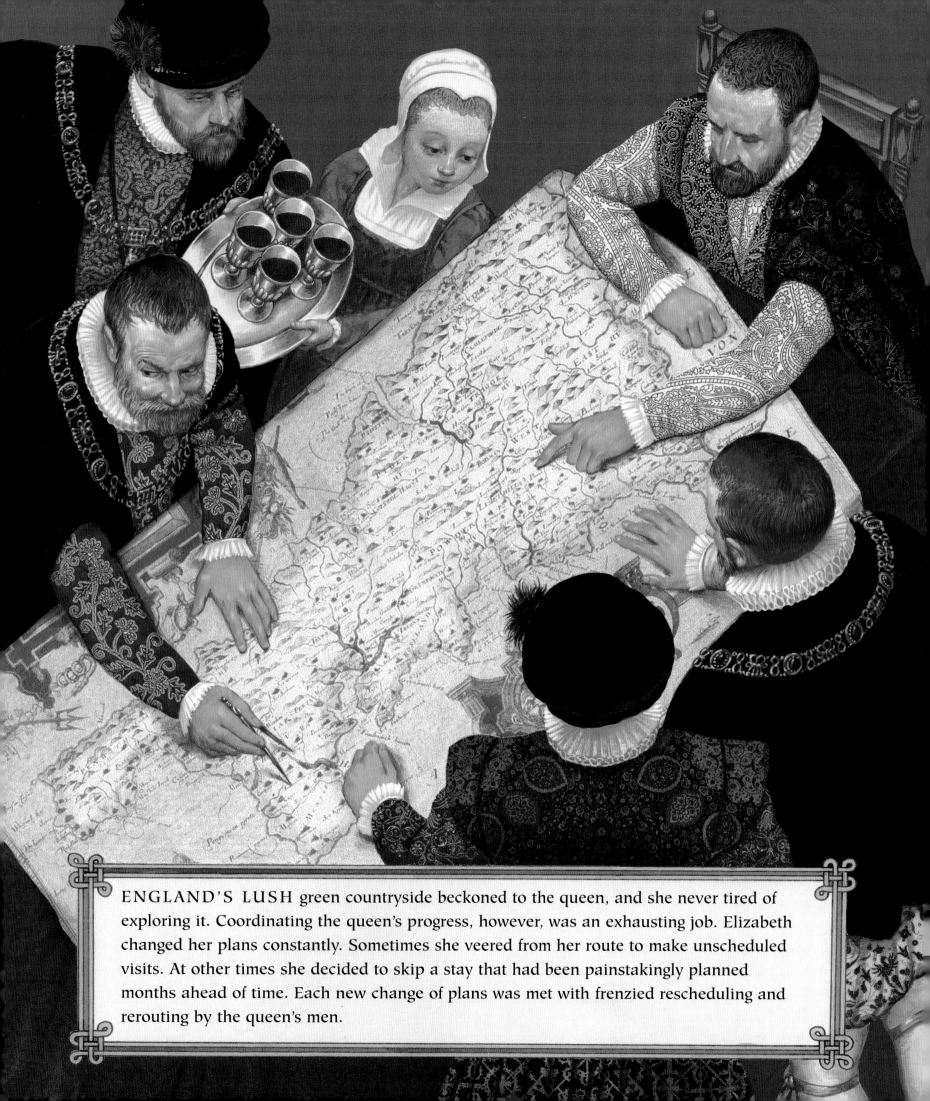

ENGLAND'S LUSH green countryside beckoned to the queen, and she never tired of exploring it. Coordinating the queen's progress, however, was an exhausting job. Elizabeth changed her plans constantly. Sometimes she veered from her route to make unscheduled visits. At other times she decided to skip a stay that had been painstakingly planned months ahead of time. Each new change of plans was met with frenzied rescheduling and rerouting by the queen's men.

F is for feast
that ends with a start.
A bevy of blackbirds
flies out of a tart!

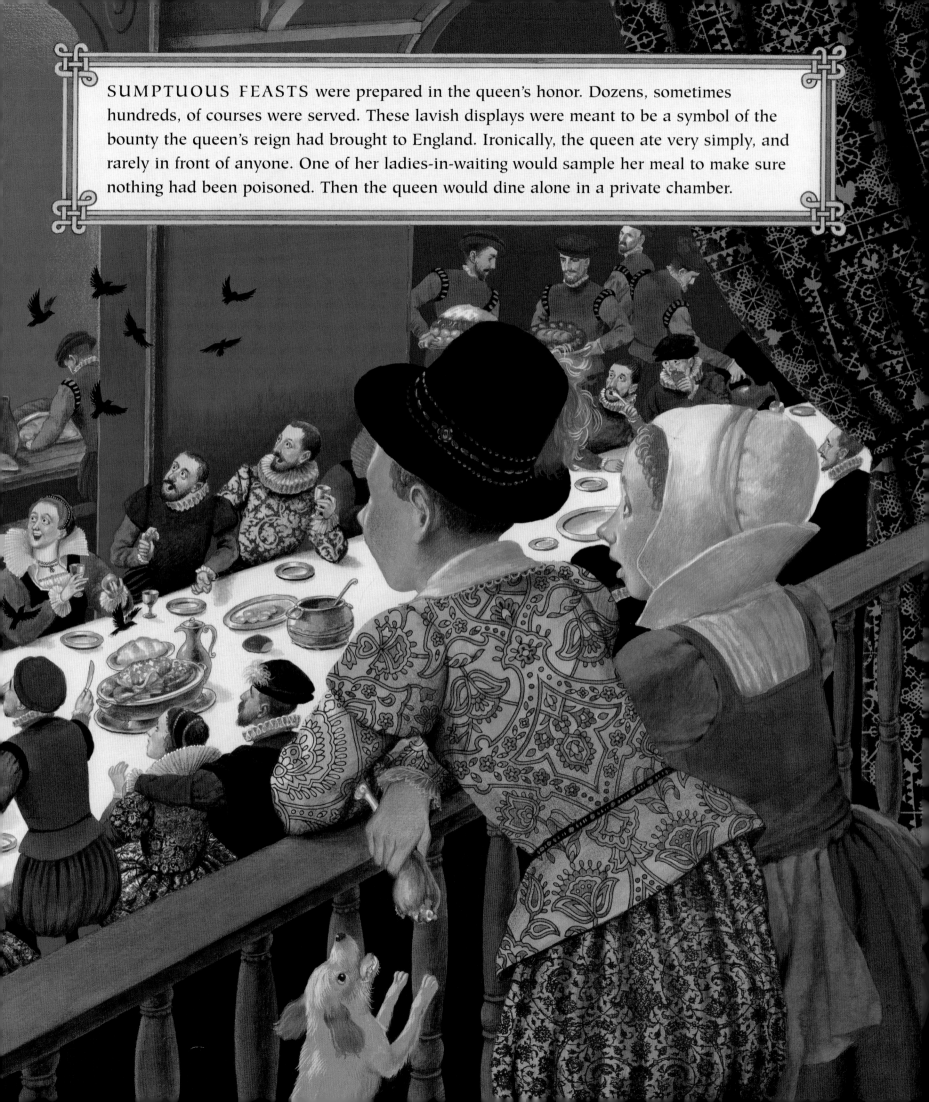

SUMPTUOUS FEASTS were prepared in the queen's honor. Dozens, sometimes hundreds, of courses were served. These lavish displays were meant to be a symbol of the bounty the queen's reign had brought to England. Ironically, the queen ate very simply, and rarely in front of anyone. One of her ladies-in-waiting would sample her meal to make sure nothing had been poisoned. Then the queen would dine alone in a private chamber.

G is for garden,
and in it a maze.
Through a tangle of hedgerows
the queen makes her way.

THE QUEEN stayed at the great houses of her nobles while on progress. As grand as palaces, great houses were often designed in the shape of an "E" to honor the queen.

Pleasure gardens were extensions of these homes, rather like outdoor drawing or reception rooms. Elizabeth frequently sought exercise and reflection in these gardens.

THE QUEEN enjoyed hunting in royal parks and the private game reserves of her hosts. Crossbows and longbows were her weapons of choice when she hunted red and fallow deer, boar, and other game. This she did from the concealed position of a hunting stand, or on horseback.

H is for hunters,
bowstrings drawn tight.
But who's the real target
as arrows take flight?

I is for intrigue,
and shadowy strangers.
The chase has begun.
Our queen is in danger!

MANY PLOTS were aimed at Queen Elizabeth during her reign. The greatest single threat to Elizabeth was her cousin Mary, Queen of Scots. Some thought that Mary was the rightful heir to the English throne. They wished to place her on that throne, sooner rather than later. Several assassination plots by Mary's supporters put Elizabeth's life at risk.

FOR MANY years Queen Elizabeth traveled in the company of Thomasina, one of her court jesters. Thomasina, a dwarf, was a well-spoken woman with an elegant bearing and a wardrobe of altered clothes from the queen's own closet. A masterful storyteller and comedienne, Thomasina often said in jest what others at court only dared to think. Queen Elizabeth, who had a quick wit and scathing tongue herself, no doubt found Thomasina a refreshing companion.

J is for jester,
who's nobody's fool.
"Threaten the throne,
and get what you're due!"

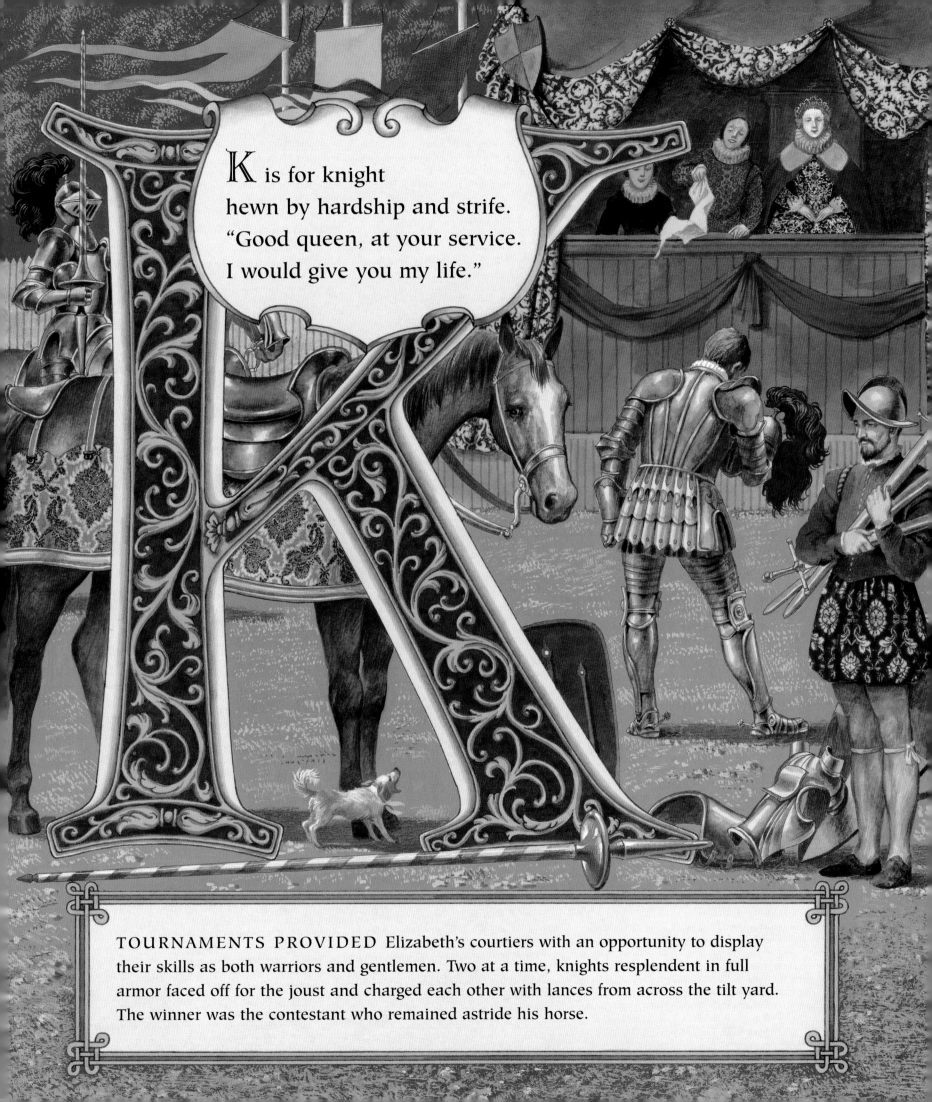

K is for knight
hewn by hardship and strife.
"Good queen, at your service.
I would give you my life."

TOURNAMENTS PROVIDED Elizabeth's courtiers with an opportunity to display their skills as both warriors and gentlemen. Two at a time, knights resplendent in full armor faced off for the joust and charged each other with lances from across the tilt yard. The winner was the contestant who remained astride his horse.

L is for ladies
who wait on the queen.
She trusts but a few.
The rest primp and preen.

OVER A dozen noblewomen waited on Elizabeth as ladies of the bedchamber and privy chamber. These ladies-in-waiting helped her bathe, brush and style her hair, apply make-up, dress and undress. They also made sure that her gowns and jewels were clean and in good repair. Elizabeth was a demanding mistress but could be generous as well. She often gave dresses and jewelry she'd worn only a few times, or not at all, to her ladies.

A CALL to the queen's service was a great honor. Roughly a quarter of her attendants were nobles, but the majority of work was considered too menial for high-born men and women to perform. Others were employed to scrub and wash, fetch and carry.

Elizabeth showed great dedication to her servants and was often reluctant to retire them, even when age or infirmity prevented them from doing their jobs well. This may have been due, in some part, to the fact that the queen spent most of her childhood isolated from her own family, and was raised instead by a family of loyal servants.

M is for maid,
called to the court
to fetch and to carry,
to launder and sort.

N is for nighttime
and nobles at play.
Faerie Queene stardust
'til dawn the next day.

EACH EVENING, entertainments took on a magical quality. Elaborate costume balls, pageants, and plays created to honor the queen were often inspired by the works of England's greatest poets and dramatists. Sir Edmund Spenser paid tribute to Elizabeth in his epic poem *The Faerie Queen*, published in 1596. In it, Gloriana, a fictional fairy queen imbued with purity, bravery, and divine right, the God-given right to rule, symbolizes the queen.

O is for orchard
brimming with treasures.
Sweet, juicy apples,
the simplest of pleasures.

MOST COUNTRY homes had at least modest vegetable and herb gardens, and perhaps a few fruit trees. Orchards were common at great houses. In the milder climate of southern England, apples, apricots, peaches, nectarines, plums, cherries, and pears grew in abundance. Fruits were eaten fresh from the harvest, pressed into cider, preserved as jams and jellies, and baked into tarts and cakes.

P is for players
who act out a scene.
Some scaffolding falls,
just missing the queen!

ELIZABETH ENJOYED performances by traveling players or actors. Players roamed across the countryside in search of a ready audience. If a theater wasn't available, they were happy to set up a makeshift stage on a village green or in the shelter of a nearby barn. Their style of theater was earthier, less refined, than the performances arranged for the queen by her nobles.

Q is for queen,
whose right is divine.
A heaven-sent ruler,
and one for all time.

QUEEN ELIZABETH'S path to the throne was a thorny one. For years, her claim to the succession was bitterly disputed, and her honor attacked. Elizabeth was imprisoned in the Tower of London briefly when her sister Mary was queen of England, accused of plotting to seize the throne. Even well into her long reign, Elizabeth met with occasional dissenters, who were both vocal and dangerous.

R is for roses,
both red ones and white.
Along the queen's path,
a welcoming sight.

A DESIGN of entwined red and white roses was popular in tributes to the queen. This design symbolized the queen's royal family tree, and therefore her right to the throne of England. The red roses represented Queen Elizabeth's relatives in the House of Lancaster. The white roses represented her relatives in the House of York. By setting forth her royal pedigree in their tributes, Elizabeth's countrymen showed their overwhelming approval of her.

WANDERING MINSTRELS were a common sight as they entertained fellow travelers on country roads, played in exchange for room and board at private homes, and performed in any town or village that would have them. The queen loved to listen and dance to music and was also a very talented musician. She played the virginals, a keyboard instrument similar to a small piano, and the lute, a stringed instrument much like a guitar.

S is for song,
artless and airy.
Plucked from a lute
as minstrels make merry.

T is for treason.
Turncoats make ready.
They slip through the square,
with daggers held steady.

IT WAS difficult to protect Queen Elizabeth on progress. As she flitted about in her caravan of courtiers and walked into crowds without the protection of her royal guards, she made herself a ready target. How easy it would be for a strident supporter of the Scots queen to attack Elizabeth in a crowded marketplace! Her councilors and men-at-arms begged her to travel less, but she ignored their pleas.

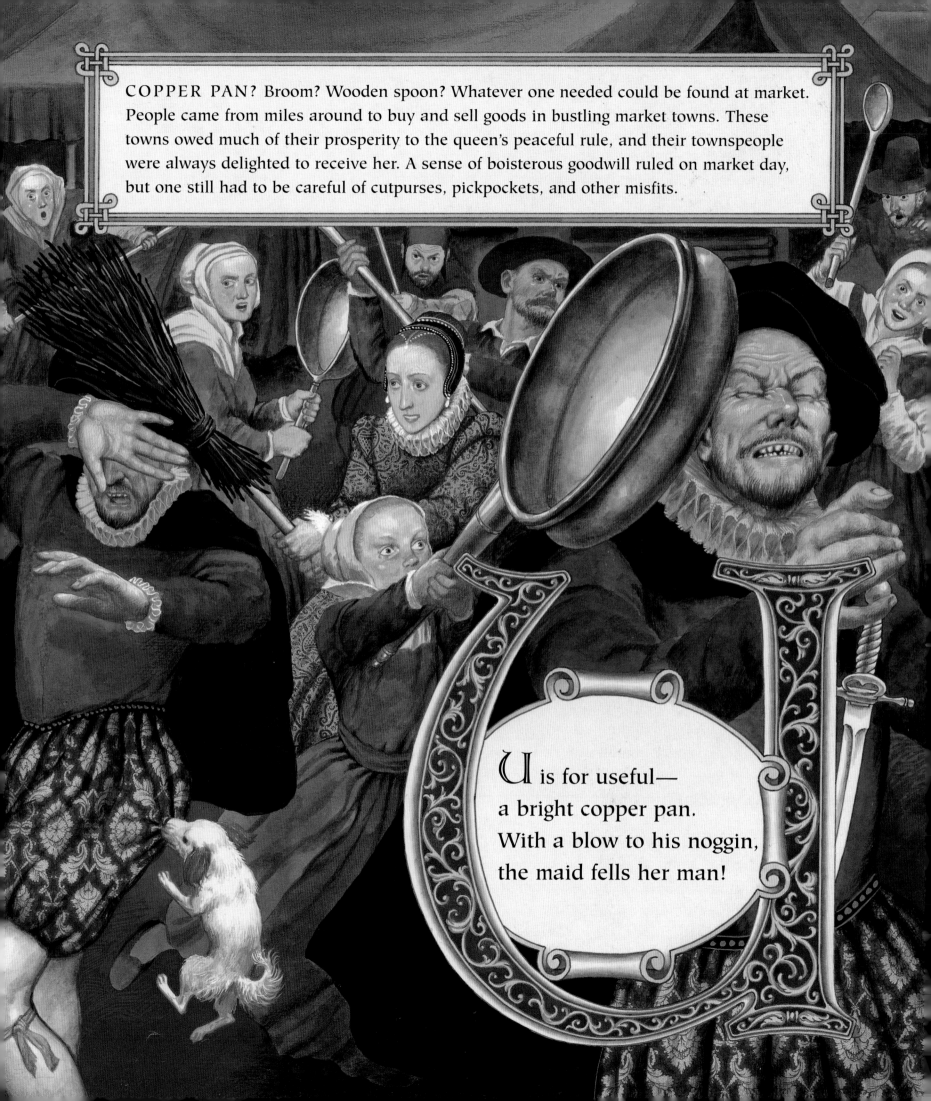

COPPER PAN? Broom? Wooden spoon? Whatever one needed could be found at market. People came from miles around to buy and sell goods in bustling market towns. These towns owed much of their prosperity to the queen's peaceful rule, and their townspeople were always delighted to receive her. A sense of boisterous goodwill ruled on market day, but one still had to be careful of cutpurses, pickpockets, and other misfits.

U is for useful—
a bright copper pan.
With a blow to his noggin,
the maid fells her man!

V is for victory.
The queen has been saved.
Thanks to a jester,
a page, and a maid.

THE QUEEN narrowly escaped plot after plot against her. She defied danger in order to walk among her people. In turn, the vast majority of her subjects gave her their unwavering loyalty. In a speech at Tilbury on August 8, 1588, Elizabeth declared:

"I do not desire to live to distrust my faithful and loving people. Let Tyrants fear. I have always so behaved myself, that under God, I have placed my chiefest strength and safeguard in the loyal hearts and goodwill of all my subjects."

W is for water,
smooth as sea glass.
The progress is over.
To London, at last.

THE QUEEN often traveled on the royal barge; a refreshing change from the rigors of overland travel. Her palaces of Hampton Court, Whitehall, Greenwich, and Richmond were all conveniently situated on the Thames River. The Thames was the greatest highway in England. From tiny water taxis called wherries to stately galleons that sailed the seven seas, the Thames brimmed with travelers and traders.

X is for xystus,
a bower of flowers.
The queen walks alone
to her ivory tower.

WHEN ELIZABETH returned to London, she met with royal duties so weighty they would have crushed most men. The queen, by choice, shouldered the weight of these duties alone. The idyllic days of summer were a fond memory to warm her through a long cold winter of responsibility.

QUEEN ELIZABETH was tireless in her commitment to England. For over forty years she ruled her country with enthusiasm, dedication, and intelligence. The royal progress, a chance to travel among her people and see the fruits of her labor, was one of her greatest joys.

Y is for yeoman
who closes the gate.
Time now for bed.
It's getting quite late.

Z is for zounds!
We have come to the end.
And now, to your dreams,
dear child, attend.

QUEEN ELIZABETH I is regarded as one of the finest monarchs in western history. She ruled England for forty-four years, dying on March 24, 1603, at the age of sixty-nine. Elizabeth never formally named a successor, but deathbed witnesses claim she said, "I shall have no rascal to succeed me; and who should succeed me but a king?" King James VI of Scotland, the son of her cousin Mary, Queen of Scots, would become James I of England.

ELIZABETH TUDOR was born in 1533, over 450 years ago. When she was two, her mother, Anne Boleyn, was beheaded on charges of treason. Her father, King Henry VIII of England, took little interest in his youngest daughter's upbringing. Elizabeth was raised by nurses, servants, and tutors in a series of households far from London and his court. She had few friends and rarely saw her half brother Edward and half sister Mary.

Princess Elizabeth made good use of her time, learning to speak Latin, Greek, French, Italian, and Spanish. She studied mathematics, religion, philosophy, literature, and history as well and was a brilliant student.

When Henry VIII died in 1547, Edward became king. When the sickly Edward died six years later, Mary became queen. It was not until 1558, when Mary died as well, that Elizabeth was crowned the queen of England. She assumed the throne on November 17, 1558, at the age of twenty-five.

The England she inherited was in a sorry state. Religious unrest pitted Catholics against Protestants, the royal treasury was almost empty, and war had weakened England's power in Europe. To make matters worse, some felt that her cousin Mary, Queen of Scots, not Elizabeth, was the rightful heir to the throne.

Elizabeth brought to bear all the intelligence and political acumen at her command to solidify her hold on the throne. She lavished gifts and favors on a chosen few, but for the most part, kept the royal purse strings tightly drawn. While Elizabeth eagerly assumed a motherly role toward her people, she would not marry, most likely to avoid sharing any of the powers of the throne. Strong and shrewd, the queen occasionally pretended to be weak or indecisive if it suited her. Feared and respected by foreign ambassadors and sur-rounded by an inner circle of canny councillors and nobles, Elizabeth enjoyed lively intel-lectual exchanges as much as she enjoyed a lively country dance.

Ultimately, Elizabeth was able to establish religious reforms and bring relative peace and prosperity to England. Her policies set the stage for an unparalleled era of cultural renaissance, exploration, and expanded British influence in the New World.

To my mother, Genevieve Grigoli Davidson, queen of my childhood
—C.D.M.

For Elizabeth and Robert Rosenthal
—B.I.

VIKING

Published by the Penguin Group

Penguin Putnam Books for Young Readers, 345 Hudson Street, New York, New York 10014, U.S.A.

Penguin Books Ltd, 80 Strand, London WC2R 0RL, England

Penguin Books Australia Ltd, 250 Camberwell Road, Camberwell, Victoria 3124, Australia

Penguin Books Canada Ltd, 10 Alcorn Avenue, Toronto, Ontario, Canada M4V 3B2

Penguin Books (N.Z.) Ltd, 182-190 Wairau Road, Auckland 10, New Zealand

Penguin Books Ltd, Registered Offices: Harmondsworth, Middlesex, England

First published in 2003 by Viking, a division of Penguin Putnam Books for Young Readers.

1 3 5 7 9 10 8 6 4 2

Text copyright © Celeste Davidson Mannis, 2003

Illustrations copyright © Bagram Ibatoulline, 2003

LIBRARY OF CONGRESS CATALOGING-IN-PUBLICATION DATA

Mannis, Celeste Davidson

The Queen's progress / by Celeste Davidson Mannis ; illustrated by Bagram Ibatoulline.

p. cm.

Summary: Uses the letters of the alphabet to provide an account of Queen Elizabeth's annual holiday, known as a "royal progress."

ISBN 0-670-03612-9 (hardcover)

1. Elizabeth I, Queen of England, 1533-1603—Juvenile literature. 2. Great Britain—History—Elizabeth, 1558-1603—Juvenile

literature. 3. Queens—Great Britain—Biography—Juvenile literature. 4. English language—Alphabet—Juvenile literature.

[1. Elizabeth I, Queen of England, 1533-1603. 2. Great Britain—History—Elizabeth, 1558-1603.

3. Alphabet.] I. Ibatoulline, Bagram, ill. II. Title.

DA355.M3155 2003 942.05'092—dc21 [E] 2002010174

Manufactured in China

Set in Hiroshige

Book design by Nancy Brennan